REVENGE
OF A
STOLEN
BRAIN

MAURICE HAMILTON

HAYMAKER PUBLISHING
CHARLOTTE, NORTH CAROLINA

REVENGE
OF A
STOLEN
BRAIN

Library of Congress Number: 2015917174
International Standard Book Number: 978-0-9839278-7-7

Acknowledgments and Dedication

*First, I want to thank God for allowing me to be used as a vessel
to speak to all those who read this book.
Thank you, Heavenly Father.*

*This book is dedicated to my family and friends who have given me their
love, counsel, and support, even during times of doubt.*

*A very special and heartfelt thank you to the editors at Scribendi,
who helped me put this story in literary form.*

CONTENTS

PREFACE

This book was written to demonstrate that being wealthy doesn't mean that all is necessarily well. It has been inspired by my own recollections, events, and perspectives obtained from my readings and viewing of many video media. While reading it, please keep in mind that it is a novel.

INTRODUCTION

Revenge of a Stolen Brain
A Novel by: Maurice Hamilton

Tragedies can occur to us at any time. Somehow, they seem to always happen at the wrong time. We may also feel that they have happened to the wrong persons. "Dear God, what are you doing? This is not supposed to happen to me. This is supposed to happen to poor people of lesser status." Sometimes, however, after a little soul searching, we learn that a traumatic experience has made us re-evaluate our values and that we subsequently gain a new insight that enables us to have a more fulfilling and joyous life.

Paul was a 34-year-old, handsome, Caucasian man. He was wealthy, well-educated, and had strong family ties and some good friends. Life was great. After all, he was born into privilege, and along with that advantage came the ability to attain most of the material things he wanted. Furthermore, he was the youngest of four, yet his father, the patriarch of the family, chose him over his older brother and two sisters to run the family's very lucrative luxury auto manufacturing business. He had a beautiful, devoted wife, Sarah, who loved him dearly and would do anything to please him. He has his whole life ahead of him and life couldn't be much better. That is, until, early one fateful morning while riding his bike— as he did every morning—he started experiencing heart palpitations, weakness, fatigue, reduced ability to exercise, lightheadedness, dizziness, confusion, shortness of breath, and finally, chest pain. He was having a stroke.

This sudden affliction changed Paul's life permanently. Although he felt very fortunate to be alive, there were times he felt like ending it all and killing himself. It was very difficult to accept that something like this could happen to him. Now, he had to deal with slurred speech, the inability to raise his right arm, and the drooping of the right side of his face. My life is over, "he thought."

~*~

Three months passed since the stroke and it was still a nightmare, until one day he got some promising news. There seemed to be a light at the end of this tunnel. Sarah did some research and learned about a new procedure called a brain cell transplant. The question Paul asked was, "Can this new technology return me to normal?" The procedure was still in its infant stages, and although there had been some successes, there were no guarantees and no way to predict how he'd behave after the operation.

He became a different person.

"Possession of material riches without inner peace is like dying of thirst bathing in the river."
—*Paramhansa Yogananda*

CHAPTER 1:
BOYS' NIGHT OUT

"Hey, Frankie, whatcha up to?"

"Hey, Blue! I'm headed to the Rack."

"You mean da one down on Pulaski and 87th?"

"Yeah, right next to that Bodega. I play on an APA (American Pool Players Association) league there and we're playing tonight around 7p.m. Why don't you come and get on my team?"

"I don't know, Frankie. I'm not that good."

"C'mon and I'll get somebody to teach you."

"For real?"

"Yeah, there are plenty of guys down there who are pretty good. We help everybody improve their game because we want our team to win and go to Vegas. Teams that win the final match will get a free trip. We could win $100,000."

"I could use that money right now! I'll go to the pool hall with you, but I have to stop by my grandma's house for a minute. I was so busy I had to work through lunch today. I'm hungry!"

"Don't worry, man. They have great food at the Rack and their Buffalo wings are half price tonight."

"Okay, but I still have to stop by my grandma's for a couple of minutes. Then, we'll go check it out, okay?"

"Yeah."

Blue's family was not very large. They consisted of his grandparents, John Beasley, who had just turned seventy-eight, and Lula Mae Beasley, seventy-six, his fifty-two-year-old mother, fifty-four-year-old absentee father, his three-year-old son, Larry III, also known as Little Blue or just LB, his twenty-three-year-old brother Tony, currently stationed in Japan while in the US Air Force, and his twenty-one-year-old sister, Goody, who had just completed a two-year program at a local community college. Blue was dating a twenty-five-year-old woman named Sheila, whom he already considered his wife, and then there was Frankie, the same age as Blue, who was considered an extended family member. There was always a financial strain making ends meet because their incomes just couldn't keep up with the rising costs of living. Chicago was an expensive place to live and one shouldn't expect to get a break just because you "lived 'n da 'hood."

"Hello, Mrs. Lou."

"Hey, Frankie," she responded, in a rather heavy voice.

"Good to see you, Mrs. Lou."

"It's good to see you, too."

Blue turned his attention to the large recliner, where John Beasley was sitting. "There's Gramps."

"Y'all come on in and have a seat."

"Hey, Gramps, whatcha been up to?"

"Oh, nothing much. Just taking it easy. I'm tired of your grandma planning for our funeral. I don't plan to die anytime soon. She acts like we's gonna die any day now. I am only seventy-eight. In the Bible, we are promised three score and ten. Each score being twenty years, plus ten, equals seventy years, but a lot of my family members died before seventy, so I gets ta live out the rest of their years. We done the wills and obituaries and now she wants me to pick five people to cry at each of our funerals. She wants one in the front pew to start it, then two in the middle pew to follow right after, and then she wants two seated in the rear pew to start and be in harmony."

"Hey, gramps, sometimes you and grandma do some strange things. How do y'all find people to cry like that?"

"Oh, that's the easy part. You see, we've been going to funerals at church for years. So, we knows all the best criers. Yeah, that's the easy part. The hard part is getting them over here to practice. Some people don't want to think about death. They think if they do, they'll die sooner than they're supposed to. I got lots of time left."

"Well, gramps, I don't believe you'll die before your time is up. But, hey, I smell something good in the kitchen; I'ma go check out what Grams is whippin' up."

Blue went into the kitchen and saw Frankie eating what looked like meatballs.

"Hey, Frankie, why are you eating all those meatballs?"

"That's okay, they're lamb balls. You can eat as much as you want. There is plenty more," Lou chimed.

"Are these really lamb nuts?"

"Yeah." Lou replied.

"What!" Frankie yelled. "Why didn't you tell me they are lamb nuts?"

She quickly replied, "You didn't ask."

"She got you, man!" Blue laughed. "But, hey, Grams, I came to give you the $50 Mama owes you. She told me to tell you thanks."

"I sure am glad she didn't forget this time. We're on a fixed income, you know. Every dollar counts in this house."

"Okay, Grandma, I'll tell her you got it."

"Okay."

"I ain't hungry no more. Watching you eating those lamb nuts killed my appetite," Blue said.

Frankie laughed and said, "Come on, man, just drop it and let's go shoot some pool. Who knows, you might meet yourself a girl and get lucky."

Blue replied, "Yeah?"

"Yeah, man. Some of them look real decent and they can shoot well, too."

"How much it cost to join this APA League?"

"Twenty-five dollars for the fourteen week session, and eight dollars each time you play. If you don't play that night, you don't have to pay anything."

"A'right, cool. Let's go."

~*~

The men reached the hall and entered a room filled with men and women practicing their craft and getting ready for their matches.

"Hey, Billie, this is my friend Blue and he wants to get on a team."

"You're in luck. Tonight's the last night to join a team and you do have an opening. You only have seven players, which gives you room for one more. Here's a copy of the rule book. It's a must read," Billie said.

"Will I have a match tonight?"

"Maybe. I'll see if I can get you in. Remember, now, that if you play tonight, it'll be twenty-five dollars plus eight. It'll be thirty-three dollars altogether."

"I understand. I am gonna pay everything now."

After watching the first two players' match, Blue was excited to play.

"Okay, Blue, you are our third player for the night. The other two players won, so let's keep our winning streak going."

After the match, Blue was looking sad and commented "I could'a beat that dude, man."

"Try again next week. It's just a fun game. Don't take it so seriously."

"Okay, I'll see you later. It's a good thing I go to work late tomorrow."

"Okay, I'll see you later."

CHAPTER 2:
TRAGEDY STRIKES

Blue and Frankie split up and walked in opposite directions. It was a cold, brisk, yet clear November night on the South Side of Chicago. Blue was on the corner of 77th and Halsted Street, just three blocks from his house. He slowed his pace when he saw a young, black, stocky man running toward him. He quickly noticed the fellow was being followed by someone in a sparkling black, 2000 Crown Vic with twenty-six-inch wheels. The window on the front passenger side began to roll down, as the driver began firing shots at the pedestrian.

Shots to the head and chest forced the man to go down quickly. The shooters spotted Blue standing there about ten feet away, frozen in his tracks. He couldn't decide whether to make a run for it or to stay put. Before he could decide, three shots rang out, hitting him in the stomach, right arm, and left shoulder.

Blue could hear the loud roaring mufflers of the Crown Vic as it quickly sped away, disappearing into the night, leaving him and the other man for dead. The sound of the gunshots and speeding car had left an eerie silence in the night. Blue wanted to get to his feet, but he could barely move. As he lay bleeding, he could also feel the strength leaving his helpless body. He could clearly see the still figure of the other fellow lying in front of him, just a few feet away, bleeding from his head and chest. He wanted to get his cell phone and call for help, but didn't have enough strength. He was able to muster enough strength to yell, "Help, help, somebody please help me! I've been shot!"

His voice attracted the attention of two couples in a blue Ford Taurus. As the car came to a screeching halt, two middle-aged men jumped out, leaving their female companions inside. Calling 911, the women were frantic as they cried for help.

"Please hurry," Blue said, in a fading voice.

Almost in unison, the men said to him, "Hang in there, sir. Someone will be here soon."

Blue began falling in and out of consciousness.

The police and ambulance arrived simultaneously. The emergency service technicians worked hard to save Blue's life. He was barely alert, but that didn't stop the police from trying to get Blue to answer as many questions as possible so they could catch those dangerous criminals.

"Who did this to you?"

"I don't know," replied Blue, in a faint voice.

"What did they look like?"

"They were two black guys in a black Crown Vic." Blue faded in and out again, and the medical techs advised the police to let them get him to the hospital, before it was too late.

"Okay," replied one of the officers on the scene, "we'll meet you at the hospital."

As they were leaving the scene, the paramedics called Mercy Hospital's triage with a short update on Blue's condition. The hospital would be well aware of the urgency and better prepared to give him the appropriate level of care.

As soon as the ambulance reached the hospital, a team of doctors began working to keep Blue alive. Dr. Glen Riemann was the lead doctor; he had the most experience in Emergency Room situations such as this one. He immediately saw how severe Blue's injuries were and asked the head nurse, "Did anyone notify his family?"

"Yes!" she replied. "They're on their way."

"Notify me as soon as they arrive."

~*~

Blue's mother, Vivian "Meme" Brown, his sister Goody, and his girlfriend Sheila hurriedly entered the hospital and headed straight to the receptionist's desk, asking, "What room is Blue in?"

The receptionist looked puzzled and asked, "Who?"

Goody quickly corrected herself and said, "I'm sorry, I mean Larry Brown, Jr."

"Mr. Brown is in the Intensive Care Unit, room number 12A," answered the receptionist. She handed Blue's mother the clipboard of paperwork to fill out.

Afterwards, the receptionist instructed them to go down the hall, make the first right, and ask someone at the nurses' station to direct them to the right room.

"Thanks" replied Meme.

With all the required paperwork completed, Dr. Riemann and his team worked feverishly to stabilize Blue's condition for the time being and to stop the bleeding. They gave him a blood transfusion.

Dr. Riemann told Meme, "We can't say for certain that any of his vital signs are stable at this time, because the damage from the bullet wound in his stomach is severe. We will know a little more if he survives the next twenty-four hours."

CHAPTER 3:
THE WAITING ROOM

Meme and Goody stood there, feeling completely helpless, with tears streaming down their cheeks. Meme gained a little composure and began thinking about what her son had told her earlier that day. After working six years with UPS, he was finally about to be elevated to a management position. He had said, "At my age, it's time I really start pulling my life together." He had been so upbeat and excited about the new position he'd been promised.

Blue usually got along well with people and was a hard worker. He thought things through and made good decisions. Meme always felt that, if given a chance, he would be a great manager. Even as a little boy, he had demonstrated many times that he had the ability to be a leader one day.

Goody looked at Meme so innocently and asked, "Why do things like this happen to good people? Blue has never belonged to a gang or gone around committing crimes."

Before Meme could come up with a reply, one of the police officers from the scene answered, "From the looks of things, he was just in the wrong place at the wrong time, as far as we know."

Goody, still reeling from the horrible news, turned to Shelia and asked, "Did you call Frankie?"

"Yeah, I called him. He's on his way."

Sheila was having her own conflicting thoughts about Blue. She had thought they would be married by now, but their relationship had been a bumpy ride over the past year. In fact, they'd just gotten back together two months prior. Blue was a great dad and lover to Sheila. He always seemed to convince her that she was the only one, but the problem was she knew better than to believe that.

She had once caught him having sex with another woman in their apartment, when she had come home from work early because of a power outage. She had been glad her employers had let her go early because she could clean up the place and maybe run a few errands. As she'd entered the apartment, she had heard a moaning sound coming from her bedroom.

She had hurriedly made her way to the bedroom and opened the door. She was shocked! She could barely get the words out of her mouth, "Blue, what the fuck are you doing with this Nae Nae bitch in my bed?"

"My name ain't Nae Nae," responded Beyonsay.

Sheila had rushed toward her, saying, "Bitch, if you don't get yo' stupid ass outta my house, I'm gonna fuck you up."

Blue had turned to Beyonsay and told her, "Hurry up and get outta here."

While Blue was apologizing, Beyonsay had quickly gotten her belongings and left.

"I've had enough of this shit; I should kill your fucking ass!" Sheila had run into the kitchen and gotten a ten-inch butcher knife. She had returned to the bedroom to see Blue's long, lean, and muscular dark body standing in front of her.

Blue had said, "Baby you are the only one I love. These hoes don't mean nothing to me."

Sheila had stood there with the knife pointed toward Blue's chest. He'd had a fully erected, ten-inch dick pointing at her big, pretty, gazing eyes. She could not take her eyes off it. She had slowly lowered the knife, put it on the dresser, and decided that she would make use of this moment and kill him later. After all, this could have been a chance to show him that she was the best woman he'd ever have. Sheila was so attached to Blue that she couldn't stay angry with him for long. After all the drama and the lovemaking, they had gotten up and driven to Chick-Fil- A for lunch.

~*~

That behavior was not unusual for Sheila. She had put Blue out of their apartment many times, but he always managed to sweet talk his way back into her life with the promise that things were going to be different. He had said that things were especially going to change now that he was expecting a promotion. Before she had let him back in the home the last time, he had proposed to her. They just hadn't set a date yet.

She certainly could have had her choice of suitors. She was a beauty pageant queen and the salutatorian of her high school graduating class. She had it all in one package: gorgeous, brains, booty, and many good friends. She had chosen Blue, who was slim, lean, muscular, six foot four, and captain of the high school basketball team. He was also smart, but not always responsible. They'd been together so long that it already seemed as if they were married.

When she'd gotten sick, it was Blue who'd taken her to the hospital and taken care of her until she'd gotten back on her feet. Although she never mentioned it, she often wondered if Blue and LB's babysitter, Regina, had been having an affair while she was in the hospital. Regina was a twenty-four-year-old, good-looking woman and she acted like she had to do everything Blue said.

Sheila had become suspicious when, just before leaving the hospital one night, Blue had told her, "I'm gonna stop by and the apartment and check on them." She really hadn't wanted him there alone with Regina. She had kept asking herself, "What's gonna happen after LB goes to sleep and the two of them are there alone?" She had quickly brushed that thought off by telling herself it was just her imagination.

There were many reasons Sheila could think of for leaving Blue, but she loved him and just couldn't stand the thought of living without him. So, she put up with his crap to keep him.

~*~

Blue's best friend Frankie was sitting across from Sheila, his mind filled with memories about Blue and their long friendship. He thought about a conversation they'd had just a couple of days earlier. Blue had said, "Man, I would love to be able to own a black 530 BMW and have some extra money to take Sheila to the shopping mall and let her buy some things she likes."

"What about your mom and Goody?"

"I'd look out for them too."

"What about me?"

"Maybe I would treat you to a night out at the strip club."

They'd both let out a chuckle.

CHAPTER 4:
STILL WAITING

Half an hour passed before twenty-eight-year-old Frankie was able to rush to Blue's side. He was completely petrified when he saw his friend lying there, helpless. Blue was like the strong older brother Frankie had never had. He could always count on Blue to bail him out during high school fights. Frankie only had an older sister, Shameka Lynn, who was a nerd in every sense of the word.

He began feeling guilty, wondering if there was anything he could have done to prevent this. He looked at Meme and cried out, "I shoulda been there! I wish I coulda been there!"

She replied, "I know, Frankie, but there is nothing you could'a done. These guys had guns and the police said they believe it was a drive-by shooting that took Blue by surprise."

Blue's dad, Larry, Sr., was also a rather tall, handsome, and intelligent man. He must have passed his womanizing traits on to Blue. Meme had tried to hold on to him for as long as she could, but finally realized that he was not going to change. They'd been divorced for ten years and had only seen one another three or four times. During the first seven years of Blue's life, Larry Sr. had stayed close and continued to help Meme with the bills, but three years ago he'd met a woman and they'd moved in together. A few months later, he'd stopped showing up, except on the children's birthdays and special holidays like Christmas, and sometimes Thanksgiving.

Things got really tough without Larry Sr.'s help, but somehow they always managed to get by. During his late teens, Blue felt like he had to grow up fast. He needed to step up to the plate and be the man of the house. He still loved and respected his dad for being there to show him how to be a man, but he wanted to know why Larry Sr. had felt he had to leave his family. As young kids, Blue and his siblings had always felt secure having their dad around. Now, Blue was forced to grow up a little faster and help Meme out with the bills. His new this promotion had given him a lot of hope.

~*~

Blue's family and friends spent the night in the hospital waiting room. Around 5:17 a.m., Meme had this strange feeling that something was not right. She awakened Goody and they went to Blue's room.

They were greeted by Dr. Riemann, who told them, "I was just about to come discuss Larry's prognosis." He told them his team had done all they could to save Blue's life, but to no avail. He gave them the sad news they didn't want to hear. "Blue only has a few hours to live."

They were devastated by the doctor's words, which seemed to echo their fears. Goody's eyes filled with tears. She hoped and prayed that her big brother would pull through. This was such an unexpected blow to their already fragile home.

Meme cried out in a whispering voice, "God, what am I gonna do?"

At that very moment, she and Goody felt a sudden calmness come over them.

CHAPTER 5:
A CRITICAL DECISION

When Dr. Reimann decided that Blue's survival was highly unlikely, he checked to see whether Blue was an organ donor and discovered that he was. The doctor knew it was time to have an uncomfortable conversation with the family.

When Dr. Riemann arrived in the room, he looked a little surprised to see the sudden change in Blue's family and he asked them if they were okay. He then indicated that Blue was listed as an organ donor and asked if they would sign off on the necessary donation forms. He assured them that there was nothing anyone could do to save Blue's life.

"There are many people waiting for organ donations. One person in particular: a wealthy businessman who suffered a severe stroke two months ago, which caused the loss of mobility in his right limbs as well as limited speech. This man is willing to pay an amount in the six figures for the donation." He explained that the family only had one hour to make their decision because Blue's brain cells would have to be removed before they deteriorated and become useless.

Meme and Goody asked the doctor to call Sheila and Frankie into the room. They were once again in tears as they tried to decide what Blue would want them to do. That was a lot of money and it could help them solve a lot of financial problems.

Since Blue's death was imminent, they concluded that donating his brain cells would be the best course of action. They believed that if he could, Blue would concur with the decision, since he had already listed himself as a donor.

They were not aware that Blue, although in a comatose state and mentally sluggish, could hear and understand every word they said. He kept yelling out, "Please don't let them do this to me! I am going to come through!" The problem for Blue was that no one could hear the words he screamed out within himself. He did manage to produce a tear in his left eye, but it was too small to notice.

Meme called her mother to explain the situation, hoping she would agree with the decision that was made.

Lula Mae went ballistic. "Child, don't let them people mess with that's boy's brain! All they're going to do is mess it up and make him crazy."

"But, Ma, he's going to die in an hour."

"I don't know what you're talking about. Here, talk to your father."

Meme explained the situation to her father. He was more reasonable. Reluctantly, he gave her the go ahead, but cautioned her to pray and ask God for his guidance and blessings. With just one person opposing, they decided to donate Blue's brain to Mr. Steuben, the transplant recipient.

CHAPTER 6:
THE OPERATION

Shortly after Blue's family agreed to the donation, Dr. Reimann gave Paul Steuben and his wife Sarah a call about the donation. Shortly after, two of Mr. Steuben's representatives, Mr. Rodney Pierce and Mr. John Swenson, came to the hospital and took Meme and Goody to their plush office downtown where two attorneys, one representing each side, were waiting to witness the signing of the donation contract agreement.

Once that was completed, the representatives drove Meme and Goody to the PNA bank and opened a savings and checking account. They deposited most of the money in local banks. Meme took $100K with her to pay some bills and buy a new car. After all the banking was done, the men took them to lunch. They drove through Paul's neighborhood first, and afterwards, to the Brown's house. Meme and Goody felt a little ashamed about these rich people seeing that they lived in the 'hood, after being introduced to Mr. Steuben's luxurious lifestyle.

~*~

Paul and Sarah headed to the hospital while his attorneys were handling the paperwork side of things, since Blue's brain cells only had so much time before they would no longer be useful. Paul was all geared up and ready for the operation, and it didn't seem to bother him that he would only be the fifth person to ever get a human brain cell transplant. Mr. Steuben's team did the research to determine which doctor would be best qualified to do this tedious and sensitive operation and chose Dr. Horace Hammonds, chief surgeon at Marcy Hospital, to perform the operation.

Dr. Riemann had been sure he would be the one performing the operation and became a bit upset at the situation. He told some of his close colleagues that he was being discriminated against and was puzzled as to why Dr. Hammonds was always chosen over him. They reminded him that during his twenty-year tenure, Dr. Hammonds had performed hundreds of intricate brain surgeries at Marcy Hospital. However, none of the previous surgeries had the same impact as this pioneering brain cell transplant. It had made international news the previous summer and had drawn inquiries from thousands of stroke patients from around the world.

Dr. Hammonds also had more experience and had proven to be more qualified. After all, he had successfully performed this operation on four other patients. Mr. Steuben specifically had requested that Dr. Hammonds do the operation. Therefore, it was not a matter of discrimination but of experience, as well as the patient's choice!

~*~

Paul quietly contemplated his situation. He was willing to try anything that could possibly reverse his current health condition. He was well aware that this technology was not one hundred percent up to scratch. He was 36 years old and earned a six figure salary as the chief engineer for body structures, safety, and development at Aston Martin. He had been married to his beautiful 34-year-old wife, Sarah, for eight years.

Sarah had it all: brains as well as beauty. She was one of the directors at the Art Institute of Chicago. They didn't have any children, but they did have a three-year-old Chihuahua. They had been good friends since junior high school. They had wonderful friends; some of which they had known since their years in junior high. They had worked hard over the years and had become financially independent.

After receiving the doctor's prognosis, Paul had been determined to reverse the effects of the stroke, get his health back, and get his life back to normal. He had refused to accept his condition from the stroke as permanent. His determination to get his health back was his priority and he was prepared to accept any consequences.

Prior to the operation, Dr. Hammonds had explained to Paul that there could be undesirable consequences if the information in the new brain cell's neural pathway was not completely blocked off. The person receiving the new brain cells could develop a dual personality. The transplanted brain cells could spread throughout the brain, causing the other person's personality to become dominant periodically. It would be as though there were two people living in one body.

On March 9th, 2012, Paul became the fifth patient to receive a brain cell transplant by Dr. Hammonds. He was the last patient in the first phase of a medical trial to determine the safety of the revolutionary procedure. The main concern was that Paul's repaired brain could take on many of Blue's personality traits. In this early stage of this new technology, brain cell transplants had not developed to the point that the doctors could control the brain function.

Just seven hours after the doctors at Marcy Hospital completed this very delicate operation, Paul was sitting up eating cherry flavored Jell-O, while eagerly waiting to discuss his prognosis with the neurosurgeon.

Dr. Hammonds appeared, asking, "How's my favorite patient feeling?"

Paul answered, "I am feeling great, Doc."

"Raise your right hand. Now, touch the right side of your face," asked the doctor.

Paul did all the things the doctor asked him to do, effortlessly. He was quick to point out, "My feelings are back!" He said this in a strong and deliberate voice. "My face feels normal. It feels like it felt before the stroke."

"That's great! But we still have to keep you under observation for another seventy-two hours before we can release you."

"Thanks, Doc, for everything. You've given me my life back, and my wife and I are eternally grateful."

CHAPTER 7:
BACK TO NORMAL

Paul was very confident that he had made the right decision to have the operation and was sure his life was getting back to normal. After six months of intensive therapy, he relearned speech patterns and how to walk. He now felt as though he had been redeemed, and had retuned back to his normal self.

Paul could now fully enjoy the things he once used to: his luxury mansion on the Southside of Chicago, driving his Steuben GF600 convertible, and participating in his former social circle. Besides the fact that he didn't have to depend on his lovely Sarah to push him around in a wheelchair anymore, he was indeed satisfied with the outcome.

"I'm walking with a new swagger," he said to himself. "There must be a God somewhere, and if there is, I thank him from the bottom of my heart for giving me a second chance to live my life."

He had more than just his health back. He now had the same surefooted and confident walk that was characteristic of Kobe Bryant. In the 'hood, they called it a swagger. In addition, his penis was ¾" thicker in diameter, 3 ½" longer, and it rose to the occasion.

Sarah loved the change and seemed to have a heightened interest in sex. Her sexual interest had been somewhat muted prior to Paul's operation. He was the one who had always initiated sex. It seemed he was oversexed and undersized. Now, he was evenly matched. She reminded him of the time he had ordered a penis enhancer from the internet and they had sent him a magnifying glass. The distributor had warned that one side of the magnifying glass would make the penis look larger and the other side would make it look smaller. The instructions had said to put the side of the magnifying glass over an erected penis to make it look larger and quickly turn out the light. This was supposed to make Sarah remember the larger penis when they engaged in sex. The problem was, Paul had put the side of the magnifying glass over his erect penis that made it look even smaller.

It hadn't been a good night. Sarah had felt sorry for him and had tried to make him feel like the sex was great. They had been together so long that he could tell when she was faking an organism. Now that he'd had the operation, that type of nonsense was a thing of the past. Paul felt that he had really lucked out on all fronts.

CHAPTER 8:
TWO PEOPLE—ONE BODY

Paul's speech and mobility on his right side continuously improved, to almost complete normalcy. This is nothing short of a miracle, he thought. He did, however, have one problem that made him feel uncomfortable: Blue.

Blue was supposed to be dead, yet he could enter Paul's mind and take control. This was a major cause for concern, but who could he talk to about it? Dr. Hammonds had already explained that there was a strong likelihood that this could happen. He had also explained that the operation was irreversible. Paul had to figure out who he could talk to, and how to deal with another man sharing his mind, body, and soul.

Paul began to have frequent headaches because he was carrying a burden of having two people living in his body. Blue now shared his brain and his body and would cross the line and do things to Paul that were hurtful. Blue, on the other hand, was still carrying resentment because he believed his life had been taken prematurely. Paul decided that it was time to get some professional counseling for his struggles with the situation and he went back to Dr. Hammonds to ask the surgeon if he had any recommendations for someone who could help Paul with his situation. Dr. Hammonds recommended that Paul speak to Dr. Raphael Jenson, who currently worked with other brain transplant recipients who were experiencing the same problem after their operation.

After six months of working with Dr. Jenson, the doctors decided that it was time to let others, especially Sarah, know what had been taking place in Paul's head. Paul told Sarah first and then he called a family meeting, where he explained to everyone what was happening to him. Sarah and the family were understanding and promised to give him all the support they could.

Paul still relied heavily on the advice and counsel from his cohabitant, Blue. Blue had given him much good advice and had shown him another side of life that he had been missing. It was because of Blue that he had a better understanding of his wife and other people. And although the car company that his family owned was still on the high priority list, the relationship with his family was now his top priority.

When Blue took control of his brain; Paul was unable to stop him. He could have a conversation with Blue, but Blue didn't always agree with him and did things his way. Paul remembered the first night he'd had sex with Sarah after the operation. Blue had taken over his mind and told her how beautiful she was, held her in his arms, and made her feel so special. Paul was fully aware of what was going on and realized that he had been so caught up in his work that he had practically forgotten to pay attention to his beautiful, faithful wife. Blue made all the right moves before making love to Sarah. He took the time to make sure she was ready.

A few weeks had passed since Paul and Blue had started making love to Sarah when Paul noticed Sarah doing strange things in her sleep. He would look over at her and see her sucking her thumb so erotically. It made Paul wonder who she was thinking about while she was sucking her thumb like that. At times, he was tempted to wake her and experience whatever she was doing in her dreams. But Paul, being Paul— routine and boring—never came to experience the erotic passion his wife was experiencing in her dreams.

It had been a long time since Sarah had felt this way. She was overjoyed that her husband was once again looking at her the way he had a few years ago. He was taking time to really make her want to make love to him.

Her beautifully carved body was on fire with passion. It was like she had become love starved. She could not get enough of his hot kisses, the caressing, and his whispers of "I love you, baby" and "damn; you are so beautiful; you are the only woman I'll ever need." He made her feel like she was so important to him. He even looked at her like it was the very first time he'd seen her naked, his eyes moving up and down her seemingly perfect curves. She could see in his eyes what he was thinking: My God, what a beautiful woman and she's all mine. She couldn't help but notice the difference in the size of his penis and she loved every minute of it.

Paul was ambivalent. He wished that he had been the one making such passionate love to Sarah, and getting that response from her, instead of Blue. Furthermore, he thought, "How dare he make love to my wife?"

At that moment in time, Paul was not so sure the operation had been a good idea. Then, he realized that without this wakeup call, he would have eventually lost his beautiful wife from neglect. Blue had clearly demonstrated that Sarah was starving for Paul's love. She was such a sweet and dedicated person that lovemaking did not require a home run hit every time they had sex. However, she did need it from time to time; all women did.

Sarah began feeling like she was making love to two different men. One was full of passion and fulfillment and the other was just performing a routine sex act; the same as it had been before the operation. She wasn't aware that it was Blue she was having sex with when she had multiple orgasms, but she surely looked forward to it. Whenever Sarah sensed that more passionate side of her husband's personality, she did little extra special things to keep him in that mood.

Paul felt both guilt and anger at the same time. It was hard to accept that he had become so routine and negligent with his wife. She had never complained and he had never noticed. He had felt that lovemaking had become routine after being married a few years. He could figure out how to rev up an automobile, but he never gave much thought to revving up his marriage.

Sarah had been his pillar of strength and had helped him become the man he was today. He was overcome with guilt when he thought of the things he could have and should have done with his beautiful wife. She was always by his side. During the first year of their marriage, they had tried to have children, but learned that they would not be able to because Paul's sperm count is too low. They decided to have a childless marriage and get a pet Chihuahua, Coco. Because of Paul's low sperm count, they didn't have to worry about Sarah getting pregnant so they just never used protection. In fact, they would have been thrilled to have a child.

CHAPTER 9:
BLUE GETS REVENGE

Paul was still brooding over the fact that Blue could make love to his wife and do it better than he ever could.

Paul had always had a very competitive nature. It was a trait he'd gotten from his father, Richard Steuben Sr. His older brother was more laid back and level headed: he got just about as much work done, but he did it with less stress. His brother knew that it was very important to balance work and family. Many people, including his doctor, believed that Paul's hard driving competitive nature was what had contributed to his stroke. He worked hard all day with very little sleep. It seemed that he believed his self-worth was validated through his accomplishments at work.

Paul decided he had to figure out a way to pay Blue back. When it was Paul's turn to be in control of the body, he paid Sheila a visit, on the pretense that he was just following up to see how they were doing. Sheila invited him into her apartment and they started out with small talk about her and her family. LB was at Gramma Lou's for the weekend.

"Can I offer you a drink?" Sheila asked.

"What do you have?"

"I have Chivas Regal or Chardonnay wine."

"I'll have a glass of wine."

After a couple glasses of chardonnay, Paul began to sound like he was Blue. He began reminiscing about the good times they'd had.

Sheila started to become frightened and confused, but she loved the idea that she was communicating with Blue. She didn't know whether to ask Paul to leave or keep him there, so she could hear more of the sweet talk from this man who sounded like her Blue. She missed Blue so much and this guy knew so much about her that he just as well could have been Blue.

The more chardonnay they drank, the more Sheila's guard dropped, until she gave in to Paul's desire to make love to her. It wasn't quite the same as it had been with Blue, but it was a close second. Sheila had not felt that way since she and Blue had made love.

Paul's visit had to be cut short. He received a phone call from Sarah, reminding him that her family would be coming over to visit.

Although Paul was not exactly the same as Blue, he did leave a good impression on Sheila and they promised to see each other again. Now, it was Blue's turn to brood. Although he had cheated on Sheila numerous times, he still didn't want anyone touching his beautiful woman. This forced Blue to call a truce: he and Paul would leave each other's woman alone. The problem now was that each woman preferred the other man. If they truly wanted to keep their women happy, Paul and Blue would have to continue making love this way.

Paul came home to find Sarah sitting on the sofa crying. "What's wrong honey?"

"It's Coco. It hurts to see her in so much pain and now it's every day."

"We both love her, but you know she's getting up in age. She's been a wonderful companion, almost like our child." Paul grabbed Sarah, gave her a heartfelt hug, and said, "We may have to put her down, honey."

They were both painfully aware that Coco was ten years old—seventy years old in dog years—and she had developed several illnesses that came along with aging: arthritis, blindness, and idiopathic vestibular disease.   After much discussion, they made the very sad decision to put her down to prevent further suffering.

Losing Coco was like losing a child. She had been such a loyal and loving member of the family for so long. She would always be loved and missed by both Paul and Sarah.

CHAPTER 10:
A NEW LIFE

It had only been a month and a half since Sarah and Paul had begun their newly rejuvenated sex life. Prior to Paul's operation, sex had just been routine and lacked the excitement they had enjoyed earlier in their marriage. They had never been more excited in the bedroom and they were now having sex more often.

The previous week, Sarah had begun feeling nauseous; she was frequently urinating, tired, sluggish, and constipated. Some of these symptoms were new, but similar to those that she had experienced just before menstruating. There were too many strange things happening, like when she started vomiting in the mornings. She decided it was time to see her doctor.

Sarah's visit to the doctor gave them another reason to be excited. He looked at her with a big smile and shouted out the words she thought she would never hear: "You're pregnant!"

"Wow! What a gift." Sarah thought she had always wanted at least two children. She began to wonder if there was still time. After all, she was thirty-two years old. Ten weeks later,

Sarah had her first ultrasound appointment and that was when the technician yelled, "You're having twins!"

Sarah couldn't have been happier. She was already making plans to take a leave from her job to be a full time mom. There was plenty of room for them in their big house and the big back yard. The schools and the community consisted of upper middle class people and the neighborhood was a great place to raise children. The sickness she was experiencing had seemed a curse, but it had turned out to be a huge blessing, above and beyond anything she had ever imagined.

Paul, on the other hand, had mixed feelings. He was very happy to have children to carry on his lineage, and he knew that kids would make his wife and the rest of the family happy. However, he did have a secret that no one in the family knew, not even Sarah. There were two people living inside his body. He thought, What if one or both of the boys act like Blue?

If this came to happen, it could threaten to change their social lives dramatically. Their white friends were not so eager to accept black people and their culture.

CHAPTER 11:
SARAH AND PAUL EXPERIENCE SOCIAL CONFLICT

Sarah had a set of unusual twin boys. The first boy came out white and everything seemed great. However, five minutes passed and another boy came out, and he was obviously a black baby.

Sarah was really puzzled and asked the doctor, "What happened? How can one child be white and the other one black?"

The doctor explained that, although it is rare, the chance it does occur is about one in a million.

Sarah really didn't care; she was so happy to be a mother that nothing else mattered. After discussing it with Paul, they named their first born Isaac and the other one Isaiah. Everyone except Paul was still shocked and surprised that Isaiah was black. Paul's brother Richard asked, "Why didn't it show up when she had the ultrasound?"

The doctor explained that a child's color does not show up on an ultrasound.

Up until this point, Paul and Sarah had lived rather simple and very private lives. Now, it seemed everyone wanted to know what had happened, making them overnight celebrities. They even had the paparazzi taking pictures of the whole family without permission. Paul had to hire body guards to protect them. Although he was a proud father, some of his happiness was dampened by all of the unwarranted attention he and his family were receiving.

Sarah couldn't even walk down the street with the boys in the twin stroller without being subjected to people staring at them and asking, "Who is the black child?"

Sarah's answer was always the same. "They are twins."

She was even followed by a middle-aged couple who stared into the stroller as though they were at a freak show. Many people questioned whether Isaiah was Paul's child. They didn't think it was possible for a white man to have a black child.

While Sarah was breastfeeding in a hotel, one of the staff members rushed over to her and told her that she had to move over to a corner. With a perplexed look on her face, Sarah asked why, and went on to explain that the blanket covered her breast. The staff member went and got the manager. That's when Sarah realized it was not about breastfeeding in public: the problem was breastfeeding a white child on one tit and a black child on the other.

Both Sarah and Paul were beginning to see that raising biracial twins was not going to be an easy task in America's racist climate. One good thing they had going for them was family support. Both Paul and Sarah's families made a conscious decision to band together and give full support at all times. There were never any problems at either of their work places. Everyone thought the twins were adorable. At least that's what they said.

Both Paul and Sarah had always wanted children and they loved the boys, but there were times they kind of wished they had stayed childless. They were unprepared for the cruelty and racism from complete strangers. They behaved as though their lives were entwined somehow. Strangely enough, things eased up a bit during the next six or seven years.

By the time the twins were six, and in first grade, things seemed to have gotten a little better; at least in their community. While shopping in the mall, people just assumed the boys were friends. It was easier that way because both Isaac and Isaiah had developed their own unique personality traits. Isaac has the same personality characteristics as Blue, while Isaiah behaved more like Paul. Neither of them seemed to have been damaged by the negative reactions they had received in their earlier years. They were both just fun-loving, rough-and-tumble boys.

CHAPTER 12:
BLUE RECONNECTS WITH HIS FAMILY

In spite of his fights with Blue, Paul was grateful for the life he had now and he knew that if it wasn't for Blue's family having made that critical decision, things might not have been so great. He decided to pay Blue's family a visit.

He called Meme. "Hello, Mrs. Brown. This is Paul Steuben."

"Oh my God, how are you?"

"I am doing fine. I just wanted to let you know that my wife and I appreciate what you did for me."

"We're glad things worked out."

"My wife suggested that I have you all over for dinner this Sunday, if you don't have any dinner plans."

"We'd be glad to have dinner with you and your family."

~*~

Meme and Goody were so excited and it just so happened that Blue's younger brother, Tony, was home on leave and he would be able to join the family. Although it wasn't obvious, Tony was just as excited as the women. He wanted to see who had gotten a second chance at life from his brother's donation.

That Sunday, Paul sent his driver, Rodney Pierce, to pick Blue's family up in one of his luxury cars—the stretch version of the *Steuben* GF800.

"Wow!" Goody took a surprised look at the unusual car and asked Rodney, "What kinda car is this?"

"It's the company's flagship car. The GF stands for Ground Flight. It is one of the first auto pilot cars and it can park itself."

The car was so comfortable and more advanced than any car Blue's family had ever seen. It even had over 300 voice commands and it responded like it was human. It didn't seem like they were riding, instead it seemed like they were in flight. Once they reached their destination, they were fascinated to actually see the car parallel park. "Wow! What a car!" Goody exclaimed.

They ended up at Michael Jordan's Steak House downtown. The host led them to a huge dining table, where Paul and Sarah were sitting having champagne. As Meme and the family approached, Paul and Sarah stood and greeted them with hugs. In unison, Paul and Sarah said, "Hi, we are so glad you were able to make it."

"We're glad to be here," Meme said. "This is such a fabulous place. I didn't know Michael had a restaurant here in town."

"Oh yes, this has been our favorite dining spot for years," Paul said.

Sarah couldn't wait any longer to ask, "How's life been treating you all?"

Meme took a deep breath and told her, "The family is still healing, but things are much better since they caught the guys who did that to Blue and they are in jail with no chance of ever getting out."

Sarah wanted to know how those guys had been caught.

Meme went into detail as if she enjoyed telling the story. She also told Paul and Sarah that they had never been to places like this because they could not afford them. Furthermore, they were always working to try to keep up with bills that they didn't have time to visit those places.

Paul promised to take them out to a few of those places during the next few months.

Once meal time was over, they all quickly drove to downtown's beautiful Millennium Park, where they had tour guides waiting to take them on a guided tour. The Browns really enjoyed seeing a side of Chicago that they had only seen on television or in the newspapers. It was a joyful experience for all of them.

Just as they had promised, Paul and Sarah returned a month later and took the Browns out to dinner. This time, they went to Gepade Caffe. It was another unheard of place for the Browns. They thought Michael Jordan's restaurant had been the ultimate eating place, but this place might just have had it beat by a little bit. The food and service was the best.

After dining this time, Sarah had scheduled a visit to her workplace, the world-class Art Institute of Chicago. There, they were treated to a family tour, where they were introduced to the institute's African collection, which included the diversity of tradition-based arts on the continent, with emphasis on the sculptural traditions of West and Central Africa. This was truly a treat for the Browns. It was also the first time they had ever visited the Art Institute. It was quite a learning experience.

Paul and Sarah were determined to keep their promise to take the Brown's to dinner each month. The next month, after dinner, they visited the top of Willis Tower for a breathtaking view of Lake Michigan. Most recently, after dining out, they took the Browns to one of their local dealerships to show the Browns all the different models of cars Steuben made, including a GF 900 SUV, a GF 600 sports car, their GF 800 flagship model, and their GF 700 coupe.

CHAPTER 13:
SNITCH DOES SOME SNITCHING

Blue's killer, Robert "Roach" Johnson, a wannabe gangster, went to prison for burglary. While incarcerated, his conscience got the best of him and he could not hold his secret any longer. He wanted to tell someone about a murder he and his friend, Charles "Smitty" Smith, had committed. For some strange reason, he felt he could trust his cellmate James "Snitch" Price. Snitch didn't talk too much and he was a good listener. So, Roach told him about the night he and Smitty had shot and killed two men three months earlier. Roach didn't know that Snitch was really a snitch, so he started to tell what happened.

Snitch saw this as a possible opportunity to gain his freedom. He had three more years to go on his five year sentence for armed robbery. He was a quick thinker and told Roach to wait until after dinner, because it was just after lunch and they had to go their separate ways for work detail.

As soon as he got a chance, Snitch made a call to the District Attorney's office and made a deal. The DA's crew came to the prison, wired him up, and sent him back to the cell. Later that night, Roach told Snitch the story in great detail about what he and his road buddy, Smitty, had done that night.

Based on the details of the confession, the DA knew they had enough evidence to get a conviction against Roach and Smitty, based on his confession, so they released Snitch and charged Roach and Smitty with the murder of Ronald Jackson, the first man that had been shot and killed. Then, they convicted both of them for Blue's murder.

Roach and Smitty were sentenced to death by lethal injection. There was some drama in the courtroom during the sentencing. Blue's dad and brother got close enough to punch Roach and Smitty in the heads before the bailiff and the court officers intervened. Larry, Sr. and Tony could have been charged with assault because they got in some good punches that drew blood. The judge decided to let them go.

The Brown family went home feeling somewhat relieved. They had a feeling that justice had been served. The men had received the death penalty because in both cases it was premeditated murder. The family met at Meme's house for dinner and to bring closure to this horrible chapter in their lives. They also let Blue know they were going to see to it that justice was done and they were all there for him to the end.

Larry Sr. gave a heartfelt apology to his family for not being there for them and asked for their forgiveness. He said he felt somewhat responsible for Blue's death.

Meme quickly interjected, saying, "You can't hold yourself responsible for that. That could'a happened, even if you were here."

Larry, Sr. also said he missed his family and wanted to spend more time with them. They all welcomed him back.

Meme later learned that Larry had type1 diabetes and was not really taking care of himself. She allowed him to move back into the house so she could care for him. That was a move that made them all happy.

~*~

Meme filled Larry in on what's been going on since he'd left. He knew about the transplant and the money Meme had received, but he didn't know that Blue was still alive in Paul's body. Before he could wrap his brains around that, he also learned that he was somewhat a granddad to Isaac and Isaiah, as well as Sheila's twin daughters, Emma and Emily.

It was all confusing, but he was thrilled to meet and talk to Paul. When Blue was in control of Paul's body, Larry knew he was talking to Blue. He had a mixed feeling of sadness and joy at the same time. He was sad that he could not see his son, but at the same time, he was glad to let him know how much he loved and missed him.

A few years had passed since Blue's funeral. Meme and Goody had moved forward in their lives. Their biggest decision was whether to keep their current house or move to a better one and start over. The Johnson family had lived in that house fifteen years. It held many good and bad memories. After much deliberation, Meme decided to buy the house they'd rented all those years. She found a good contractor who made all the repairs and added a sunroom as well as a deck. She also managed to keep some money in her savings account.

Goody was very happy with her mom's decision to stay in the neighborhood near their grandparents and old friends. Grandma Lou was also happy. She told Meme that leaving their home and moving to another neighborhood would not be a good idea at this time. She believed that Blue's spirit would always be in that house.

CHAPTER 14:
RACISM RAISES ITS UGLY HEAD AGAIN

May 15th was Founder's Day for Steuben Motors. The company had been founded by Richard, Sr on that day in 1964. Many eyebrows were raised when Paul skipped the range of dishes that were usually prepared for this important event. The guests included the who's who of the luxury car industry and they were used to selecting from a menu of lobster BLT, dover sole with orange miso vinaigrette, and beet latkes with pastrami duck and apple mustard, smoked salmon, chicken pot pie with shaved black truffles, sautéed German sausages with bacon and apple sauerkraut, roasted rack of pork with sausage stuffing, warm potato salad pancetta and brown butter dressing, braised chicken thighs with sauerkraut, and a variety of traditional deserts.

This was the worst time for Blue to make an appearance. Instead of the lavish menu already prepared, he requested fried chicken, collard greens with ham hocks, black eyed peas, and blackberry cobbler.

A little more than eyebrows were raised when Paul said he was going to donate $10M, to be distributed among five

Historical Black Colleges and Universities (HBCUs). No one, except Paul, understood why he was making these radical decisions.

Paul came to the realization that he was going to have to share his body with Blue, so they agreed on certain boundaries. First and foremost, Paul demanded that Blue stay out of his and Sarah's sex life. He didn't want another man having sex with his wife, even if it caused her to have more orgasms. Blue agreed because he had a strong intuition that, sooner or later, Sarah's body would crave for him to make love to her. It was the way he looked at her while she'd dressed and especially when she was naked.

CHAPTER 15:
WILL PAUL AND BLUE MAKE PEACE?

Although Blue agreed to stay out of Paul's sex life, the feeling of doing something forbidden or taboo fueled his excitement to new levels. The lovemaking between Sarah and Blue was never routine. The excitement starts the moment she woke up, beautiful and desired by her husband. It built to a crescendo, like that in an orchestra, as she thought about him throughout the day. Paul never took the time to show that he cared about her the way Blue did. Their sex life had become boring and infrequent. Since his operation, a breath of new life had been blown into their sex life.

Blue also agreed to stay out of Paul's business and personal life. Paul realized that these boundaries were necessary because Blue was doing things that were completely out of Paul's character. He bought condoms and left them in his office desk. Paul had never cheated on Sarah, so there was no need for condoms, as far as he was concerned. Furthermore, he had a very low sperm count, so there was no fear of getting anyone pregnant. Unfortunately, Paul didn't figure out what Blue had in mind until it was too late.

Two days had passed since purchasing the condoms. That Wednesday, after lunch, Paul was sitting in his office when his secretary, Allison McGuire came in to consult with him about a business-related letter. Unfortunately, Blue had taken over the body and Allison was not aware of the situation.

Blue asked her, "Hey, Allison, is your father a baker?"

"No, why did you ask that?" Allison responded.

"Because you have some beautiful buns."

She smiled and was pleasantly surprised that her boss finally recognized her beautiful, well-carved body.

Approximately ten minutes later, she came back into his office to let Paul check and see if the letter was written to his specifications. As he was reading the letter, Allison sat next to him, a little closer than usual and showing more of her thighs than usual. She could feel the sexual energy building fast between her and them. They stood up, hugged, and kissed each other. The lustful passion was growing fast, as he ran his hand up between her thighs. She opened her legs and welcomed his caressing hand moving slowly between her voluptuous porcelain white curves. It led to her very warm and wet, hairy pussy. She took off her panties and opened her legs to allow him to come in between them and enter her wet pussy. It was quick and Paul stood looking at her apologetically.

She looked at him as though she was saying, "DAMN! Why did you wait so long to do this?" and "Why did you come so fast?"

Blue had once again satisfied his sexual fantasy and disappeared into the background, leaving Paul to deal with any damage control. Paul looked at Allison, apologized profusely, and pleaded with her to keep this a secret.

She promised it would always be their little secret.

CHAPTER 16:
PAUL REFLECTS ON HIS LIFE

After Blue's reckless escapade, Paul began reminiscing about his childhood. His mom had always been accusing his dad of cheating, and he had made a vow never to cheat on his wife because he could see the pain it had caused his mother. There were six of them in the immediate family, Richard, Sr., his mother Phyllis, Elizabeth ("Liz"), his older brother Richard Jr., and younger sister, Jacqueline ("Jackie").

Richard Sr., a highly decorated Vietnam veteran, was definitely the patriarch of the family. He professed to have strong religious convictions, but he struggled in the area of womanizing. He lived what he was taught by his WWII veteran father, George. He was taught that men are supposed to dominate and control their environment and the people they deal with. He went to work in a grey flannel suit and believed that women were subordinate to men and should stay home as housewives.

Paul's father was a five foot nine, medium built, blue eyed man with receding blond hair and a thick gray mustache. He was a staunch, conservative, Roman Catholic Republican. He ran his household similar to the way he ran his business, except at work he would have meetings for all plans to be shared and discussed. At home, however, he just told everyone what to do and how he wanted it done; their feelings didn't matter. This included his wife, Phyllis, who stood 5'6" tall, and had hair that had turned completely grey. She convinced her husband to let her have her hair dyed a soft blond; she had it dyed religiously every two weeks. She didn't get to do many things that she wanted because Richard questioned everything she did. He didn't think women had the same mental capacity to make good decisions like men could.

When he died at 54 from a massive heart attack, his wife had been relieved and felt a sense of freedom that she hadn't known since being married. She felt throughout their marred marriage that she took a secondary role to the business. Although she tried very hard, she came to the realization that she would never be able to please her husband. As she reflected back, she concluded that her life with Richard had been dull and she would always have been his doormat. She decided that the rest of her life would be fun filled. She went out often with her friends from church to play bingo. They occasionally went to the casinos in Vegas and Atlantic City; they created a widows' group.

The children kept an eye on her, just to make sure she didn't become too extravagant. They were surprised to see her choose their GF600 sports car. She also changed her wardrobe; her style of dress made her look younger. She went to the gym and worked out three times a week, joined a walking group, and lived her life happily ever after.

Phyllis met Robert Benson at the gym and began seeing him. Robert was a six foot tall, blond, handsome man, who always dressed well. He was also a local bank president.

Over the first year, their relationship developed into a very strong friendship.

One day, while her oldest daughter Liz was visiting her, Liz asked her mother, "Mom, you've been seeing Robert for quite a while. I don't know if I should ask you this, but I wanted to know if the two of you are sexually intimate?"

"Liz! How dare you! I don't discuss your sex life and I am sure as hell not going to discuss mine with you! I asked you over to have some of the pineapple cake and peach lemonade your sister made. Let's stick with that."

"Yes, Mom, but I just—"

"Stop it! I am not going to discuss this with you. Robert is a very nice man who treats me with respect and we like each other very much. That's all you need to know."

"Okay mom." Liz took a sip of the punch and exclaimed. "Wow! This really is good."

When Liz left the house, she still wondered about what kind of relationship her mother was having with Robert.

~*~

Richard had been really disappointed that he'd had a girl child before having a boy. All the children were two years apart. This meant that although Liz was two years older than Richard Jr., the leadership role in the family went to him.

Liz resented this and, as a result, she rebelled against her parents, causing her to become the black sheep of the family. She didn't try to live up to the expectations her family had for her, but instead, made her own. It might have had something to do with the fact that although she was the first born child in the family, Richard seemed to give the boys more of his attention, and gave them the leadership role over the girls. By the time she was fourteen, she was drinking liquor left in the glasses when her parents had guests over for a few drinks and a game of cards. At seventeen, her drinking had escalated to a point where she began to steal it from the liquor cabinet. She started high school as a straight A student. Halfway through her senior year, she was barely passing. Her parents donated a great deal of money to the school and used their influence, to make sure Liz graduated.

When she and her high school sweetheart, Derek Huff, got married, Liz was twenty-two years old and already four months pregnant. She knew her religious faith forbade pre-marital sex, but she did it anyway. She never finished her college degree, which was a requirement for all the children by her father. Yet again, Liz chose the path of most resistance.

On the other hand, her sister Jackie only drank with her occasionally. She wasn't as much a rebel as Liz, but she did like to have a little fun with her older sister. It didn't bother her as much that the boys received more attention. She made lots of friends outside of the family and was involved in after-school activities and had managed to become the captain of the girls' basketball team, as well as the leader of the school's debate club. She didn't have any long term relationship with boys until her second year of college. That's when she met a six foot tall, blond-headed, soft-spoken young man named Charles Rittenhouse, who was to become her husband.

All of Richard's children worked for the family-owned auto company, Steuben North America, Inc., as did the husbands of both his daughters. Their flagship car was the Steuben GF 800. The interior of this car looked similar to the 2015 Bentley Mulsanne model. However, that's where the similarities ended. The GF was an auto-piloted car that could also park without assistance. While traveling, one would rarely ever feel bumps in the road because when riding in the GF, one was not just riding; one was having a Ground Flight, (GF). It also had an optional sensor that enabled it to avoid most accidents.

CHAPTER 17:
LIZ AND DEREK FIND A SOLUTION

Liz and Derek continued to drink alcohol to the point where many times they did not show up for work. Richard reluctantly fired Derek because he believed that the man should be the bread winner, but Derek's drinking problem gave Richard no choice but to release him.

Derek blamed Liz for his drinking problems, stating "Before I met you, I did not have a problem with alcohol. You drink so much and I just wanted to please you by joining in on your drinking festivities."

Although she didn't like the fact that her father had fired her husband, she took pleasure in knowing that she could come in from work and yell at her two teenage daughters and at their father, as if he was a teenager too.

At some point, when Liz was sober for the entire day, she began thinking about some of the bad things she had done from the results of drinking. Both she and Derek had left the children home alone when they were about three or four years of age, more than once. Jackie had stepped in many times to ensure that Lisa and Caroline were safe during the times when Liz and Derek were not fit to take care of the girls. She also remembered that the family had held cookouts and other gatherings, leaving Derek and herself out because of their drinking. She truly did not want this kind of life, but felt hopeless and did not know where to turn for the help she and Derek needed.

The day after, Liz had a few drinks while at work and made several errors. That was when her father made it very clear to her that if she and her husband did not rectify their drinking problems, he was going to fire her and write her out of his will.

Liz knew her father was serious. She went home and she and Derek drank more vodka. They laughed and talked about killing her father before he had a chance to change his will. They fell asleep, she on the couch and he on the living room floor.

The next day, around 7a.m., Liz woke up with a terrible hangover. She managed to sit upright on the couch and stare down at her husband, who was still on the floor in a fetal position. His face lay in his vomit. She thought to herself, "This has got to end."

She went into the bedroom, opened the drawer of the nightstand on her side of the bed, and took out the loaded 38 caliber pistol. She headed back down stairs to shoot Derek and kill herself. Just before she reached the bottom of the stairs, she missed a step and fell headfirst onto the floor. The gun went off, waking Derek in the process.

"What happened?" Derek asked in a slow, slurred voice.

"Oh, nothing, I was just putting the gun away and it fell and went off."

Liz got up and quickly took the gun back upstairs and put it away. Just as she put it the drawer, the phone ring.

"Hello?"

"Hello, Liz. I was thinking about you and wondering what if anything I could to help you and your husband. I did some digging and found this program that might help both of you."

"What kind of program, Jackie?"

"It's a program called Alcoholics Anonymous. They are people who have drinking problems and the help and support people suffering with the same problem."

Liz and Derek looked for Alcoholics Anonymous groups in the yellow pages. Derek had lost his driver's license as a result of driving while intoxicated. He also really wanted his job back, and to be a father to his daughters. He was happy to finally arrive at a state of hopefulness. He was willing to try anything that could help him get his life back and get him back on the right track.

Liz and Derek attended their first Alcoholics Anonymous meeting and made the decision to move forward with correcting their lives by attending on a regular basis. They both celebrated their fifth year anniversary of sobriety and regular attendance at Alcoholics Anonymous. They made every effort to make restitution to both of their parents, friends, and creditors.

Richard died in their third year of sobriety, but he, his daughter, and son-in-law had developed a good relationship. Before Richard passed, he realized that his decision to spend a great amount of time with his sons had hurt Liz deeply. He told her that he now understood how it made her feel, and that it had been wrong for him to do so; he didn't know any better, and he sincerely asked for Liz's forgiveness.

From that point forward, until he died, they had a great father-daughter relationship. Derek received his job back from the company. Their two daughters, Lisa and Caroline, attended Al-Anon meetings, which was a program for relatives of alcoholics that helped them to be able to cope with their loved ones' addictions and how to support them. Jackie and Charles also attended the meetings, and the entire family attended occasionally. They were all anxious to learn how to cope with addiction and learned that alcoholism is a disease, and that Liz and Derek were not bad people. The two had a drinking problem and needed help. An understanding of the disease made it easier for the family to forgive Liz and Derek and to move on as a family.

CHAPTER 18:
PAUL AWAKENS TO SARAH'S NEEDS

Paul began to realize the very poor relationship he had developed with Sarah. For the 10 years they'd been married prior to his transplant, they hadn't had any children because of his low sperm count. They were basically living separate lives. He was very caught up in his work, and spent very little time with her, except for the occasional business functions when he needed to show her off. Sarah had adjusted to that lifestyle and had buried herself in her own work. She managed to ward off temptations from her male colleagues, and other men she met in passing, because she was determined to be faithful to Paul.

The experience of sharing his body and mind with Blue gave him a completely different outlook on life. When Blue became the dominant person in the body, he paid attention to all the details, big or small, when it came to Sarah. She responded like a person starving for love. She didn't realize that all the attention and passion was not coming from Paul, but from Blue. Paul was grateful that Blue had taught him how to be the type of husband that Sarah desired. What he was not happy about was Blue having his way sexually with his wife. He often thought to himself, I wish I could kill that motherfucker. He shouldn't be fucking my wife.

Paul knew that he couldn't kill Blue, because killing Blue would be killing himself. For the past five years, Paul had allowed a lot of resentment against Blue to fester and at some point he knew he was going to have to get rid of those resentments or his life would continue to be miserable. He kept recounting what Blue had done since he'd come into this body. Blue had made passionate love to his wife, to the extent that she enjoyed it more with Blue then she ever had with him. He'd screwed Allison, Paul's secretary, and got her all riled up. It could have been very expensive and problematic, if Allison had been the type to use blackmail against Paul. Blue was a great guy; however, he did some things without realizing that there were life-changing consequences to his actions

Paul also spent a lot of time thinking about all the good things he had done for Blue, in an attempt to make things work out between them. After all, Blue had given him his life back. One of the things he was considering, as a way to get back at Blue, was to stop giving millions of dollars to the historical black colleges and universities. He also threatened to fire Blue's old girlfriend, Sheila, and stop payments on the new house he had bought her.

On the other hand, both women experienced immense pleasure every time they made love. Normally, Paul would not have cheated on his wife, nor would he ever have had sex with a black woman. However, to get back at Blue, he decided to charm his way into Sheila's bed. Both women made him feel manlier than he had ever felt before. Paul realized that five years was far too long to carry resentment; so now he was taking Blue's advice and he bowed to his knees and asked God to remove it.

It was important to lose his resentment towards Blue, especially since he had fathered another set of twins with Sheila; Ella and Emma, who were five years old. Both girls were very intelligent and their personalities were very similar. In fact, it was hard to tell one from the other, sometimes.

Paul, with Blue's help, had managed to make both Sheila and Sarah happier than they could have ever imagined. It also made him happy, for the most part. He never thought he could have children, and was always insecure because of his small penis, but now he had four children and a dick big enough to keep two women satisfied.

At one of the company's dinner parties, Paul was sitting at the table in the middle, along the side instead of in the middle up top. He motioned for everyone to be seated; and for his secretary to come sit with him.

Allison quickly noticed the difference in the seating arrangement and asked Paul, "Why aren't you on stage, in front of the audience, at the podium, like the leader?"

Paul replied, "It doesn't matter where I stand, Allison. I am still the leader."

Despite the negativity towards the menu, only chicken bones were left on the plates, and there were no complaints about whether the food was healthy or not.

CHAPTER 19:
MIDDLE SCHOOL TROUBLES

Both of Paul's boys tested high on the IQ test administered to them at the prestigious Lincoln-Douglas Middle School, where they were placed into the top classes. Because of their heights and great athletic abilities, they also joined the 7th grade basketball team. None of the students at LDMS realized the two were twins until their feet hit the court. You could tell they practiced together all the time, from their flawless execution and knowledge about where the other was on the court at all times. On the basketball court, their color difference didn't matter.

Yes, there were questions like, "How is it possible to have a black sibling when both parents are white?" or "Is that really your brother?"

When they answered yes, the response was always, "But that's impossible."

Although the boys were basketball stars, not everyone liked them. Often times, kids would call them liars. Isaiah and Isaac grew tired of the harassment and started showing people they were twins instead of constantly telling them.

The trouble for the twins escalated to the point where Sarah and Paul were at their wits' end. At the age of eleven, both boys had already earned black belts in Martial Arts, so they defended themselves well. Paul and Sarah had to go to the school almost daily because parents complained that their sons got black eyes from one or the other of their boys.

Most of the hatred was directed at Isaac, a white kid claiming he had a black brother. Although he was slightly smaller, Isaiah always came to his brother's defense. Paul and Sarah didn't know what to do in this situation, but they knew there had to be a way for their sons to go to school without getting into fights.

They never thought it would be a big issue sending their biracial twins to this prestigious school. After a long discussion between them, Paul sought advice from Blue, who had become his best friend, advisor, and counselor. Blue suggested that they transfer the boys to a different school. After all, there was a plethora of highly rated schools in Chicago.

What they now had to decide was whether to send them to a private school, some of which offered Advanced Placement (AP) and International Baccalaureate (IB) courses as well as impressive college placements for graduating students. Those schools also offered small class sizes, where students enjoyed personal attention from their teachers, and a variety of extracurricular activities and athletic choices.

Another option for Isaac and Isaiah was a parochial school, which offered faith-based education to its students. While these schools offered all the same benefits of a traditional private school, the boys would have the opportunity to participate in religious practices in addition to the academic curriculum. This could be the best choice because there would be less concern about the difference in their color and more emphasis on giving them the best educational experience possible.

Before making any final decision, Paul and Sarah discussed the situation with their extended families, who agreed that a parochial school would be the best route. The boys were transferred to Mind Extension Academy, near Lincoln Park, which had a better test score rating and was more integrated than Lincoln-Douglas. Here, Paul and Sarah believed the boys would be judged based on of their academic and athletic achievements, rather than their bi-racial relation.

CHAPTER 20:
FROM BOYS TO MEN

During their high school and college years, Isaac and Isaiah dated girls from different races. Isaac's prom date was a black girl and Isaiah's date was a white girl. They both went on to finish high school and college with honors. They both received advanced degrees in mechanical engineering before joining the Air Force. They both met and married women they'd met in college. Isaac married Michelle Williams, a very brainy and beautiful African American woman who had a degree in Art & Design. Isaiah married Brittney Madison, a very beautiful and intelligent white woman who also had an advanced degree in Art & Design.

Things were going well for the Steuben family. Isaac and Isiah were now working for the family company. Paul and his brother, Richard, took the boys under their wings, as well as Richard's son, Josh. They were working on a new design for the Steuben GF800. They were preparing this car to use autopilot and other advanced technology. They would not be the first to use this technology; however, they could be the first to enable it. The Steuben GF800 would be the first car to drive on auto pilot. It could also avoid accidents, and park itself.

CHAPTER 21:
PAUL REVEALS HIS SECRET TO SARAH

Paul had been carrying heavy secrets from Sarah ever since he'd had the transplant. It had been a torturous two years for him. There came a point where he needed to come clean to Sarah, to let her know why he behaved the way he did at times. This was one secret he could no longer hold. After dinner one night, when the house was empty and quiet, Paul grabbed a bottle of their favorite wine and decided it was time to let Sarah in on his well-guarded secret.

He explained to her that he felt hurt and disappointed at times when they were making love and didn't know how to explain to her that Blue was sharing his body. He divulged to her that Blue had the ability to take control over him at times. Paul explained to her that he was angry because Blue sometimes took over his body when they would make love and it was Blue who had brought all the passion into their sex life.

"It angered me because I didn't want any other man to ever touch you. On the other hand, he made me realize how much I have neglected you."

Sarah put both hands to her face and leaned forward with tears in her eyes, as Paul moved closer to her and wrapped his arms around her. She then moved her hands from her face and embraced him back. Sarah began "It doesn't matter. I still love you, and you've given me all I needed from this marriage. We have two beautiful sons and we still make great love. To me, it's not Blue: "It's you who's making love to me."

Paul felt a tremendous relief but hesitated for a few minutes before he dropped another bombshell. He said, "I have one other thing that is very important for you to know. I was so angry with Blue for making love to you while using my body that I wanted to get revenge in any way that I could. So, I went to Shelia's apartment one night and had a few drinks with her. Once the alcohol kicked in, I was able to recall important pieces about Blue and Shelia's relationship. Shelia was impressed enough that we were able to go all the way. We had sex that night. It happened on several occasions and eventually Sheila became pregnant with our twin girls, Ella and Emma."

That was a bit much for Sarah to take in. She stood up and smacked him across the face, saying, "How could you!"

He grabbed her arms and explained to her, "Hey! It's important you know the truth. I only did this to get even with Blue. But the girls are here and they are a part of me and I love them just as I love my sons. It would mean the world to me if we could save our marriage and I could still have a relationship with my daughters."

Sarah walked over to the wine bottle and refilled her glass. Pacing back and forth between the living room and dining room, she tried to make a decision to throw Paul out of the house or accept his news and move forward with their marriage. She asked him to sleep in the guest room for the night, while she tried to figure out how to move forward. She needed to be alone.

~*~

The next day, while having breakfast, Sarah told Paul that she would accept his wishes to keep a relationship with his daughters, as long as he promised to never have sexual relations with Sheila again.

"It wouldn't be me making love to Sheila, it would be Blue," Paul explained. "Remember, we're two people living in the same body."

Sarah looked at Paul and said, "I'll try, Paul."

Paul then got up from the table, hugged Sarah, and with tears in his eyes, said, "Thank for understanding. I love you so much. I would never do anything to hurt you."

They both decided that this was a sacred covenant between them. It could not be broken nor did they want to revisit it in the future.

CHAPTER 22:
ELLA AND EMMA LEARN ABOUT RACISM

Eventually, Ella and Emma met their half-brothers. From that day forward, the girls were invited to Paul's house for family dinners and gatherings. They became a well-adjusted and blended family.

Although they were biracial, Ella and Emma did not experience racial problems at the same level that Isaac and Isaiah did. As far as Paul was concerned, beauty and race were concepts that societies create that might not actually exist in reality. To him, both girls were very beautiful by any standard. However, on many occasions, they were treated differently by some of their white classmates and by some adults. While in secondary school, they even went through identity crises. Their 8th grade art teacher, who believed they were Spanish with American names, would often say things like, "¿Cómo estás? or ¿Qué día es hoy?"

Sheila reminded them that they were black.

Ella quickly corrected her and said, "You're black, Mom. Dad is white and we are brown."

Sheila decided that it was time for her daughters to learn about the rich heritage and culture of black people. She made sure to add an African American History class to their schedule of classes.

CHAPTER 23:
RECONCILIATION

After coming clean to Sarah, Paul realized he and Blue could no longer do vengeful things to each other. The two decided that since they were two people living in one body, if they were going to survive, they needed to cooperate with each other. It was no longer just the two of them being affected by their petty games. It now included four children, Sarah, and Sheila, who had a vested interest in the families' survival.

Blue made the first gesture and told Paul, "I was very angry with you because of what transpired at the hospital. All I wanted was revenge and you gave me that opportunity by keeping me alive in your body. I am done with that now. We have four children and it's time for us to think about them, your wife, and Shelia, instead of just ourselves. I am very sorry for what I did to you and I am very sorry for the way I made you feel, but put yourself in my shoes. I believe you would've done the same thing."

Paul then apologized to Blue for what he'd done with Sheila to get revenge. He went on to say that he had learned a lot from the experience, including how to be more attentive and passionate to his wife. He also learned to have more respect for people of color. "This probably would have never happened if I didn't have you in my life," he admitted. "Prior to my stroke, I was spiritually bankrupt and out of touch with people in general. Today, I can truly say my family and I have never been happier. Blue, you are an important part of my life. I couldn't have done it without you."